LOVE. ACCEPT. BELIEVE.

TRAILER /

Trash

R=THINK PRESS

First published in Great Britain 2018
by Rethink Press (www.rethinkpress.com)
© Copyright Mike Elliston

Supported using public funding by

ARTS COUNCIL
ENGLAND

LOTTERY FUNDED

Cover design by Tanja Prokop

Acknowledgements

TRAILER/trash is the result of many years of writing, researching and re-drafting. I wouldn't like to put a figure on which draft this published version is – but it's a high one! It's also the final one.

Writing this play hasn't been a lonely process. Instead, I've had the good fortune of working with numerous theatre practitioners who, over a number of years, have helped me put it on its feet, from a self-funded production in 2012, after which I let it settle for a while. In 2015, I received funding Arts Council England (ACE) to re-develop it as a research piece in collaboration with an outfit I have since come to admire and respect tremendously, The Salon: Collective. That redrafted version saw one character "Dottie" completely reinvented as "Shyanne", while Frankie was redrawn into a more credible, non-binary younger person wishing to transition from female to male. This published script is the one I am now satisfied with for full production and once again, I am grateful to the additional funding received from ACE for making that possible.

I am also incredibly grateful to the friends, family and individuals who chipped in with top up cash donations that allowed me to place it in front a live audience in Cambridge at the Hotbed Festival in 2015 (following a highly successful script-in-hand performance at London's So & So Arts Club) but also to the many people who have followed me and this play's long dirt road, and the others I have since turned out, as I rekindle my career as a playwright. These friends and supporters each embody TRAILER/trash's call to action: Love. Accept. Believe. That's how you make me feel about myself and my work. And that's how I feel about each and every one of you. Thank you.

Finally, I am indebted to both Lucy McCarraher and Joe Gregory at Rethink Press who, through their generous sponsorship, have made the publication of this script possible.

TRAILER/trash
by Mike Elliston

This version of the script was premiered at The Quarry Theatre at St. Luke's, Bedford, UK on 10th April, 2018.

Cast

Frankie	Isabelle Bonfrer
Shyanne	Rayna Campbell

Production

Written by	Mike Elliston
Director	Dominic Kelly
Asst. Director/Stage Manager	Preece Killick
Design	Kevin Jenkins
Lighting Design	James Pharaoh
Co-Producer	Alex Vendittelli
	(for The Salon:Collective)

Notes

The play is written for two actors in the roles of FRANKIE and SHYANNE who between them role play all other characters featured in the script.

Characters

FRANKIE – early 20s, white, non-binary, assigned female at birth, hoping to transition to become male at some point in his life. Raised in traditional Bible belt community, upstate Texas, he has been denied the freedom to explore and live with his male identity by both family and church. Finally, he has run away from home to face an uncertain future when he lands up in Odessa, TX.

SHYANNE – African-American, mid to late 40s, who gets by as an 'exotic dancer' in a seedy run down club, Odessa. Her early life was one of constant disappointment and abuse. She has learned her lessons the hard way and is a survivor, clinging onto her dream of being discovered and becoming a star in Las Vegas, just like her angel cards tell her.

For my dad, Len.

ACT ONE

SCENE 1

1999. Night. Odessa, Texas.

FRANKIE makes a call at pay phone booth. He's tired,
cold and hungry. And scared. After a moment –

FRANKIE: Hi, hi, hi mom. It's me. F-F-Frankie.

> *(A long silence)*

> I, I, I was just c-c-calling to s-s-say...

> > *(The phone connection is cut. The air is*
> > *killed by the dead line.)*

> ... sorry.

He holds the receiver away from his face – bewildered and
carefully wipes the phone receiver with his handkerchief
and replaces it. He picks up his heavy backpack and hoists
it onto his shoulder. Somewhere, we hear the sound of a
heavy metal door slamming shut.

SCENE 2

FRANKIE: My folks named me "Frances Alice Anne-
Marie", 'cos in the eyes of God, I was born a girl.
But you know what? I'm a boy. So, screw you if
that ain't to your liking. 'Cos I always hated being
a girl. Like, when so-called Aunt Flo and Cousin
Red first came to stay, and I learned all about
riding the cotton pony. I felt so scared, and alone.
When my puppies showed up, I didn't want 'em,
they didn't belong to me. Uncle Pete called them
his "fun bags". I hate Uncle Pete. After worship
one time, I told my daddy, not for the first time,
"I'm a boy". He pinned my arms to my sides,
shook me so hard, and yelled "I will NOT raise a
freak under my roof, so help me God!" Even the
pastor took turns at shakin' me out. He mighta
even broke into tongues, I dunno, but then again,
he had a fat upper lip and always sounded kinda
strange. I wriggled myself loose "I hate Barbie
and I wish I was Ken! And I hate them ribbons
mom scrunches in my hair!" And by the way,

she'd tie them real tight, like, with her arthritic

claws, all twisted and gnarled, diggin' her nails

into my scalp, like a turkey vulture picking at

its prey. "I hate being a girl and…" That's when

daddy strook me across the face and dislocated

my jaw. They told the ER I'd slipped on ice.

It was the middle of August. They all turned

a blind eye. For the next nine or ten years, my

life was one big fat lie, they made me live like

their little girl. God prevailed, and all the while

I wanted to kill myself. Home was in Turkey,

upstate, along with one hundred and twenty

six other God fearing families. As a bird, the

turkey's quite big. But as a dwelling, it's on the

small side. No place for the likes of me to hide,

most times I stook out like a donkey's boner

in spring time. Except this year, on Bob Wills

Day, when every April, ten thousand folk flock

to the Texas Swing music he invented. By the

way, it's crap. This was my time. Momma's laid

up in bed, her arthritis attackin' her hips, daddy's

runnin' around her like the good Christian he

is, so I take my chance. I shear off my hair, pull

my cap down and I mingle. Invisible at last.

And, Lord forgive me, I've stuffed momma's

whole month's anti-inflammatories into my

bag. Not to make her suffer, no; just so's the

pain distracts from me not being around. I

hitch a ride with a trucker crossing State.

And I land up in Odessa, where he tosses

me out of his cab 'cos I won't blow him.

SCENE 3

Night. The sound of the city. A seedy city sidewalk, outside a strip club. FRANKIE, agitated, picks up his knapsack where it's been flung to the ground.

FRANKIE: Yeah, fuck you, too! And when I get one of my

own, you can blow that instead! Asshole!!

SHYANNE, big sunglasses, big hair, baggy T-shirt, leggings, pulling a small suitcase on wheels, hums to music on her Walkman cassette player. She smokes. The Trucker beeps his horn at her as he passes by. She angrily pulls the headphones from her ears and flips off the driver as he passes.

SHYANNE: Want some? Fifteen bucks! Lo-ser!

(She approaches the pay phone, ignoring FRANKIE. She drops a quarter into the slot. A moment.)

Yo, Melvin, it's me... ha ha ha... I'm running late. I had errands to run.... Melvin... are you for real? That is just fail in my book. No, you stay in your lane! You what? Huh? Ho? I ain't nuttin' like those jer-jer-jer-jer motherfuckin' ratchet hos you frequent with, you ugly toad. Why'd you have to say that, huh?... Why you so fuckin' messy, so fuckin' retarded messy? You just as stupid as fuck, what is wrong with you, huh? Er, jer, jer, jer, jer - the same old lame ass shit! I'm reachin' a ten here, you are so retarded... Aww, have I hurt your feelings, Melvin? Huh? You're just dramatic the whole damn time. Man, stop making me triggy, 'cos when I walk through that door I'm gonna whip your... Uh-huh. That's right. You're gonna regret treating me like waste matter on your shoe... yeah, 'cos one day I'm gonna be up

on a real stage in front of a real crowd. Uh-
huh, that's right, you heard me, what's that?
'Cos my angel cards told me, that's why.

> *(laughs)*

Well, is that so?... the longer you keep me
talking pumpkin, the longer you gonna wait
to see this bitch get her titties out. Mmm-
mm. That's what I thought. See you in five.

> *(She hangs up)*

Prick.

FRANKIE: Excuse me, you gotta light?

SHYANNE looks at FRANKIE with curiosity.

SHYANNE: You gotta dick?

FRANKIE: Sorry, I can't find my (lighter)...

FRANKIE puts a hand in his pocket to feel for a light.
SHYANNE feels immediately threatened and grabs his
arm. FRANKIE is terrified. SHYANNE softens and
relaxes, lights his cigarette with the tip of her own.

SHYANNE: Wanna come inside and see the show?

FRANKIE: Sorry, ma'am. Ain't got no money for stuff
like that.

SHYANNE: Well, shit a dick! Been a while since no

motherfucker's called me "ma'am"...

You a boy or a girl?

SHYANNE puts a hand on FRANKIE's groin and we see inside his head.

FRANKIE: Urrrgh! What am I gonna say, fuck, how I'm gonna act, fuck, what am I gonna be? Oh, shit, what if she...?... down there? What she thinking? Do I sound like a girl? Do I look like one? Oh, fuck, c'mon be a man. I'm the man. I'm the man... I'm scared.

> *(A moment later. FRANKIE looks at SHYANNE blankly.)*

Frankie. My name's Frankie.

SHYANNE: Did I you ask you your name? Wanna go bumper-to-bumper?

> *(Frankie recoils.)*

You one of them shy diesel dykes?

> *(She grabs FRANKIE's hand but he pulls it away.)*

You got outta town callous hands.

Lookin' for one of them bi-curious femmes to make scissors with?

(Back inside FRANKIE's head.)

FRANKIE: I need to puke.

(He tries to vomit.)

Ma'am, I have no idea what
you're talking about. Sorry.

SHYANNE: Jeez, you really *are* from outta town. You on
a va-gay-tion get away from the stinking
cattle? 'Cos I can smell bison off you. No
bumpin' onions with me, kid, whatever you
are, 'cos I don't do tricks for free. Go home.

FRANKIE: I can't!

SHYANNE: You still here?

FRANKIE: I got no place to go. I wasn't tryin' to trick
you. Sorry.

SHYANNE: Talking to the hand.

FRANKIE: My daddy wants me dead.

SHYANNE: Busy, busy, busy.

FRANKIE: No. Really he does. He's tried, but I jumped
outta his way, just in time. And that's the
truth. Jeez. I can't believe I just told you that.

SHYANNE: Are you shitting me? Are you shitting me?

FRANKIE: I swear, he tried to kill me with his John Deere

Ninety Five Hundred.

SHYANNE: His what?

FRANKIE: It's a combine harvester, ma'am, a beast with
your back turned to it, like I had.

SHYANNE: What kinda daddy does that? Maybe he
didn't see you?

FRANKIE: He saw me and he wants me gone, 'cos I'm...
an "abomination" before God.

(The impact of this hits them both.
SHYANNE looks at him curiously.)

That's why I baled. Before he turned me
into one. I'm sorry, ma'am, this has nuttin'
to do with you. That's all I do. Spend
my whole life apologizing for being the
who I am, when I have no idea of the
who I am, I am. I'll be going. Sorry.

SHYANNE: I got no time to for no boo-hoo hokey history
of yours. You ever done massage?
You do know how to massage?

FRANKIE: You mean, like hookers do?

SHYANNE: Jer-jer-jer, excuse me? Like what?

FRANKIE: My daddy says that's what hookers do.

SHYANNE: Is that so? Well ain't daddy the motherfuckin'
expert? Now you listen here, kid, I get paid
to dance. I'm a professional entertainer. And
call me crazy, but I'm willing to overlook that
hay bale horror, but that's the last time you
call me a "hooker". You get me? Oh. And
the massage? That was for me! Every fibre
and every bone in my body is killing me.

FRANKIE: I'm sorry, ma'am, I didn't mean to offend.

SHYANNE: What age are you?

FRANKIE: Twenty five and a half.

SHYANNE: I asked you a question. Don't fuck with me.

FRANKIE: Twenty one. Thirty six days ago.

SHYANNE holds out her hand, impatiently. FRANKIE
nervously pulls out his driver's ID.

SHYANNE: You're legal, at least. Frances, huh?

FRANKIE: Frankie. It's Frankie.

> *(SHYANNE shows him the ID, because*
> *that's not what it says.)*
>
> By the way, that's a mistake God made.
>
> I'm Frankie. My name is Frankie.

SHYANNE: That's so fucked up, whatever. Frankie it is.

So, here's what we're gonna do, kid. For one
night, and one night only mind, you get to
be my personal assistant. But that's it, don't
get any ideas, I ain't gonna be momma, you
get me? No. Momma. I don't do momma.

FRANKIE: I already got a momma...

SHYANNE: No, back up, momma talking. One word
of advice. Inside the club, sit tight, speak
to no-one and whatever you do, don't
make eyes with any of them creeps.
Especially Melvin. *Especially* Melvin.

FRANKIE: Who's Melvin?

SHYANNE: The boss, so called, fat assed jack-ass. Keep
away from his clammy eye line.

FRANKIE: I need a job, ma'am, I'm desperate.

SHYANNE: *You?* Dancing? Nude? I don't think so.

(She laughs, cruelly)

When you get through them gates of hell,
only refer to me as "Amethyst". Got that?

FRANKIE: Amethyst. That's nice.

SHYANNE: For the customers, only. That's show business.

FRANKIE: What's your real name?

SHYANNE: Think I'm gonna tell you that?

SHYANNE exits. FRANKIE hurriedly picks up his backpack and follows.

SCENE 4

Night. SHYANNE's trailer.

Lights slowly reveal a clapped out old trailer, a curtain blind hangs over the door. Two grubby movie theater seats, beer crates, discarded liquor bottles, clothes strewn around, a bucket, carry out food boxes, picnic table and a refrigerator hooked up to the electric supply. Twinkle lights adorn the trailer. FRANKIE and SHYANNE drinking beer and eating popcorn.

FRANKIE: Shyanne. That's such a pretty name.

SHYANNE: Whatever. A name's a name.

(She snaps her fingers)

Ain't that so?

An awkward pause.

FRANKIE: You were awesome, tonight. In the club.

SHYANNE: Er, jer-jer-jer-jer. You saw the show?

FRANKIE: I needed a pee and I took a wrong turn.

SHYANNE: What did I tell you? Keep your head down

and sit tight. Jeez, I'm workin' working

my way up to seven with you, already!

FRANKIE: Sorry.

(An awkward pause, then -)

Melvin, such a jack-ass.

(Imitating MELVIN grotesquely)

"Hey, Ameytits, table fifteen, upside down

long john! Go squirt, or I'll butt punk

you on the way home"

SHYANNE laughs.

SHYANNE: You sure got him down to a tee. But I got

him wrapped round my pinky, know what

I mean? Such a creep. They all are.

FRANKIE: *(imitating a CLUB CUSTOMER)*

"Hey princess, wanna give my moustache a ride?"

SHYANNE: Like I'm some kinda two dollar hollah.

FRANKIE: *(imitating MELVIN)*

"Hey Ameytits, table two, dirty kazoo!" I ain't

ever seen a lady do that before. Cool beans.

SHYANNE: You think?

FRANKIE: Straight up. Except for the guys.

SHYANNE: Butt ugly, most. Stinking breaths. Small

dicks rubbing at my ass. Twelve bucks to see my

tits for the price of a beer. I'm a black Friday pussy,

every day of the week. Guess we all just working

though our shit in there... Did you see my tits?

An awkward pause.

FRANKIE: You gotta nice place, here Shyanne.

SHYANNE: Er, jer-jer-jer-jer! What did I say about

getting ideas, kid?

FRANKIE: Sorry.

SHYANNE: This is my home. Just me. All by myself. By.

My. Self

(An awkward pause.)

So, like, when you jack off, you thinking

of a guy or a girl? I got liquid cramps

figuring you out. You do jack off?

FRANKIE: I, I, I...

SHYANNE: Clam jousting, mixed meat? You like girls?

FRANKIE: No. Yeah, maybe.

SHYANNE: Guys?

FRANKIE: No. That would mean I was a...

(Ashamed, whispering)

'faggot'. And I'm not a

   (Mouthing)

'faggot'.

SHYANNE: From where I sit, I'd say mixed up dyke.

   Look on the bright side, write some

   sad fuck country music and retire

   to the mountains. Who cares?

FRANKIE: Me. I need space, I need time, to figure it all

   out, to figure me out.

SHYANNE: You farmyard femmes are all the same, a real

   pig's breakfast.

   (Frankie pulls out a handkerchief and

   wipes his eyes.)

   Go right ahead, you boo-hoo-hoo about it.

   (Crassly imitates FRANKIE)

   "I'm so ho-ass shit all the time, so

   watermelancholy, what's wrong

   with me? Boo-hoo-hoo."

   (She kisses her teeth)

   You any idea what it's like to be me most times?

SHYANNE takes two beers from the refrigerator and

hands one to FRANKIE, who handles it nervously.

FRANKIE: Huh?

SHYANNE: Didn't think so. Try shopping with black,
           kid, downtown minority hills.

FRANKIE: I have no idea where that is.

SHYANNE: Didn't think so. Take a look, kid, far as your
           eye can see, that's where. Your problem?
           You so figgity, you forget, outside the waffle
           house, you're still Miss Six O'clock.

FRANKIE: No I ain't - even if I did know what the
           heck that means.

SHYANNE: You go anywhere you want, anytime you want,
           pussy pants. I show up, it's a whole 'nuther story.
           Security, on my tail; leaving the store, searched;
               (Reaching a nine, suddenly)
           I get held against my will for a box of potato
           patties 'til I pull extra ID outta my purse.
           One day, kid, they gonna regret that ten
           sixty six shit they pull on me, 'cos this 'nigger
           bitch', she's gonna be a star. It's gonna me
           they pay their blue collar white dollar for,
           me looking straight down the lens calling
           the shots, crushed velvet and diamanté, all

the way. Right now, I can't get even credit!
Fuck that, Miss Six O'clock! Like it or not,
you and Julia Roberts, you got a lot more in
common, and I don't mean 'Pretty Woman'.

FRANKIE: My name is Frankie.

SHYANNE: Sure. Tahtas up top, pink wrinkle below
and cinnamon ring behind. You got gas,
candy and soda all under one roof, you're
the d-r-e-a-m 7-Eleven, that's what you are.
I'd kill for one second to be you. Instead,
you cry babying, you hate your poor little
white bitch life s-o-o much. Ha! Ha! Ha!
So messy. King mess, that's what you are.

FRANKIE: I don't blame you, ma'am. I hate myself most
days. I speak like a girl, think like a boy. I can't
win, it's a long road losing streak and somehow
it's all my fault. What the hell was God thinking
when He made me? Was He depressed?

SHYANNE laughs cruelly, FRANKIE is agitated.

FRANKIE: I think I should go. I'm the 'freak' who
ruined your day, 'Miss Vivian'. I'm
real sorry. I always fuck up.

SHYANNE: You a real binger bang down.

FRANKIE gets up, ready to leave.

FRANKIE: Yup. That's me. Maybe I'll lay me down on
the turnpike and... be crushed. Yeah, yeah,
that's what I'll do. Or I can knife myself,
if I had one, or, or... you know what? I can
swallow all my momma's pills, take the pain
away, that's what I'll do. It's for the best.

SHYANNE: Toto popo poop.

An awkward pause.

FRANKIE: Good night, ma'am... by the way how much
should I pay you?

(SHYANNE throws him daggers)

For the popcorn, I mean? I don't mean
nuttin' weird by that... sorry.

SHYANNE: Wah wah wah, whatever.

FRANKIE: Have it your own way.

SHYANNE: Whatever, wah wah wah.

FRANKIE lays a dollar bill on the ground.

FRANKIE: It was real good to meet you, Amethyst,
Shyanne, whoever the real you, you is.
And I'm real sorry about...

(SHYANNE holds up "talk to the hand".)

Thanks again, ma'am.

FRANKIE goes to leave. SHYANNE waits a beat then turns around sharply, wipes away a tear.

SHYANNE: Whoa! Did I say you could go, Frankie Panky? Did I say?

(FRANKIE turns. An awkward pause.)

You had me at ma'am, you motherfuckin' king mess, you. Fuck you. Just one night, mind, one night.

FRANKIE: I don't know what to say - can you really mean that, after...?

SHYANNE: Don't push me.

FRANKIE: That's... awetastic!

SHYANNE holds her hand up to indicate "enough".

SHYANNE: Bladdah bam de bam! Grab me another beer and one for yourself. It's been a long night, already. My noodle is doodled.

FRANKIE: This is unbelievable!

(Suddenly serious)

Sorry, ma'am, where I come from, we don't like to drink so much, as a rule.

SHYANNE: Boy! God sure had it in for you when He
cooked you up, didn't He? Musta sinned badlio
last time round, kid. Psycho? Rapist? Republican?

(SHYANNE pats the seat next to her.
FRANKIE sits.)

Why all the guys I meet like soup sandwich?
Blessed angels, can you answer me that?

They drink in silence for a few moments.

SHYANNE: What you gonna do, donkey?

FRANKIE: I dunno. I need to lay my hands on some T
real soon, that's for sure. That's "T"
for Testosterone, by the way.

SHYANNE: No shit. How you gonna get yourself some
of this 'no shit' T?

FRANKIE: Cash. Lots. Two hundred a month, I reckon,
cash I don't have. Guess Frankie's gonna
live with Frances, maybe forever.

SHYANNE: That is so defeatist. Listen, I got a plan.

FRANKIE: A plan? What kinda plan?

SHYANNE: My kinda plan, that's what.

FRANKIE: A plan for you?

SHYANNE: No, for you, numbskull.

FRANKIE: For me?

SHYANNE: That's the plan. Reckon I can get you a job.

FRANKIE: At the club? I thought you said...

SHYANNE: No! *No*! Numbskull! Not the club. Why

would you be putting your tits

and hoo-ha out in the club?

> *(FRANKIE mimics some moves, comically.*
>
> *SHYANNE laughs.)*

Got my ear to the ground, I know a

vacancy going at the Sunny Side diner,

Cottonwood Drive. Know it?

FRANKIE: No.

SHYANNE: Run by Alvin. He's hirin'. Know him?

FRANKIE: No. I'm new in town.

SHYANNE: That's right, you're new in town. I get the

cloud sometimes.

FRANKIE: Who's Alvin?

SHYANNE: Alvin? Chicken fried smelling creep, about

so tall, two hundred and sixty pounds I guess,

Snicker bar for a dick, a dead dog's breath and

teeth short of a gator's bite. He owes me.

FRANKIE: Think he'll take me on?

SHYANNE: Sure. I can be very persuasive, me. Else Mrs
          Alvin's gonna shred his nuts to coleslaw when
          she finds out his shit on Tuesday nights.

FRANKIE: Tuesday nights?

SHYANNE: She's busy prayin', Hallelujah Boulevard,
          he's busy playin', Gynecology Row. Know
          what I mean? Reckon that vacancy's
          got your name written all over it.

FRANKIE: A job! For real? I can't believe it!

SHYANNE: Believe. We all got dreams, kid. And one day,
          they gonna come true. Else, what's
          the point to all this shit?

          *(SHYANNE pulls a cigarette from her
          carton.)*

          You gotta light?

FRANKIE lights her cigarette.

SCENE 5

*The trailer. Night. A few hours later. SHYANNE, seated,
holds a pack of angel cards to her heart.*

SHYANNE: Beautiful Angels, my blessed Angels,

Momma Moonshine here, checkin' with y'all.
Listen up. Guide and protect me; show me the
right and one true path for my greater good.
And for fuck's sake, give my reading clarity.

*(She shuffles the pack, spreads them on
a velvet covered small table with some
crystals and a small angel figurine. A small
vase of flowers nearby. She selects two cards
and crosses one over the other.)*

Is my time coming, is Momma Moonshine's
destiny about to unfold - know what I'm saying?

*(She pulls out the bottom card, refers to the
guide book.)*

Fuck. That long? Then answer me this. I got a
new person in my life. Frankie. Is this gonna
work out good for me? Or is it gonna be messy?

*(She pulls out another card, studies it, and
refers to the guidebook.)*

Jesus fuck.

SCENE 6

Months later. Alternates between The Sunny Side Diner and The Strip Club.

FRANKIE getting ready for his shift. He takes off his top and looks at himself in disgust. He adjust his chest binder and puts on his work polo shirt and cap. He strikes a series of manly poses.

FRANKIE: Good to her word, Amethyst 'persuades' Alvin to hirin' me and before long, I've got a couch for a bed in her trailer, and I gotta a job. And she's right about Alvin - chicken fried smellin' creep. Twelve month on, and he's even uglier than he already was.

ALVIN: Hey, he-she! Quit tuggin' your invisible dick and move your ass. Table fifteen! Service!

FRANKIE winces.

FRANKIE: Most days, I try to ignore him. It's just a job, and he's just the pay check. And I keep tellin' myself, one day, no-one's gonna speak to me like that again. 'Cos no-one speaks to guys that way.

SHYANNE transforming into Amethyst. We see her apply
her lipstick, check her eyelashes, adjust her tits, pushing them
up, etc. When she's ready, she looks at herself in the mirror for
a long time. She strikes a sexy pose.

SHYANNE: One day, baby, you're gonna be a star. Hey,

Melvin, Melvin! What's with the delay?

You said you'd sort this. How'm I gonna be

beautiful surrounded by all this shit? Huh?

MELVIN: Think you a rack city chick? Lick my nine,

bitch. You lucky I don't stick that

pole right up your ass.

SHYANNE: You lucky my sweet meats keep you and your

camel knuckle riding high.

FRANKIE: *(Turns to 'customer')*

So that's one fried shrimp and double dream

pancake. You got it! Oh, there's a delay of

ten minutes on the shrimp, is that OK?

(Turns to another 'customer')

Uh-huh. Sure, uh-huh, so that's one low

fat ranch - uh-huh, yep, on the side, you

got it. You want biscuits and gravy with

that? Sure, no problem, you got it.

SHYANNE: *(Turns to 'customer')*

Hi handsome. Ain't seen you in here before?

Is that so? Just passing through? OK.

Can I do, what was that, for you? Squirt?

Sure. Just keep your hands to yourself.

FRANKIE: Oh, we use squirty cream for that, is that

ok? Uh-huh... uh-huh... uh-huh... Want it black?

Sure, no problem. Small, regular, or large? Uh-

huh... uh-huh... uh-huh. You want something

to start to go with that? No problem. What was

that? Sure, I can get you more sugar, no problem.

SHYANNE: Sure, sugar, I can do that, no problem, but

that's gonna be fifteen dollars. And

that's just for starters. Mmm-mmm.

FRANKIE: Sir, did you want a starter to go with that?

DINER: Not from your hands, freak.

FRANKIE: Excuse me? What was that, sir?

DINER: You heard me, 'son'.

FRANKIE: Only my daddy gets to call me "son", sir.

DINER: He blind as well as dumb?

CREEP: I've seen some vaginasaurs in my time,

but you still all woman! I wanna suck your titty.

SHYANNE: All woman? Maybe so, but I ain't yours, now
           hands off!

DINER: We don't want your sort here, you and your
           disgusting ways. Crawl back under that rock
           where you came from. Oh, does that offend
           you, boy? You gotta a problem with that?

FRANKIE: Well, maybe I do, sir, 'cos I walk this way
           and I talk this way and I dress this way,
           'cos I was born this way. You gotta
           problem with that?

DINER: You better not use the men's rest room when
           I go pee. Or you got something stuffed
           down your pants you wanna show me?

*The two are now very close to each other – each feels
threatened by the other.*

SHYANNE: I said! No. Touching!

FRANKIE: You better back off, sir.

DINER: Or, what?

                    *(The DINER sniffs FRANKIE "Silence of
                    the Lambs" style.)*

           I can smell your... pussy.

FRANKIE: I'm gonna have to ask you to leave, sir.

The DINER grabs FRANKIE's crotch and with the other hand, he rubs his breasts suggestively and aggressively.

DINER: Seems like you got bulges in all the wrong places.

The CREEP grabs SHYANNE and is rubbing his hands over her tits. She slaps him and pushes him back, forcefully.

SHYANNE: I ain't telling you again, you little creep. No man-on-can action allowed. Save your dick beaters for the fries.

CREEP: Save your breath, eye cabbage. Girls half your age and half your price ten blocks away.

He spits at her.

DINER: I'm gonna tear your ass open and show you what a real man does.

He lunges at FRANKIE again, but is surprised to find himself in a headlock.

FRANKIE: What you gonna tell your wife? That a boy or a girl did this to you? You lay hands on me one more time, I'm gonna slice your dick off with a steak knife.

SHYANNE is caught in a head lock by the CREEP.

SHYANNE: Melvin! Melvin!! You gonna deal with this

                    dumb ass motherfuckin' retard asshole, or

                    what?! He's got a blade, for Christ's sake!

FRANKIE: Alvin's gonna serve your balls up for breakfast

                    tomorrow.

DINER: Says who? Me an' Alvin go way back.

SHYANNE and FRANKIE break free from each other,

FRANKIE brushes himself down. SHYANNE turns

her back and struts off but not before she turns at the

customer, a rage in her eyes.

SCENE 7

Later the same night. A payphone.

FRANKIE: But Alvin, that guy, he was just being mean

                    and rude and horrible to me, I wouldn't talk to a

                    dog that way. ..What do you mean? I don't wanna

                    stay home tomorrow and cool off! Alvin, I need

                    the money, I can't afford to lose a shift 'cos of some

                    dumb asshole... What "changes"? Alvin?... shit!

The line is dead.

SCENE 8

The trailer.

The next morning. The sound of crickets prick the silence.

After a few moments, FRANKIE emerges from the trailer.

He drinks milk from the refrigerator and spits it out. It's

sour. He checks the inside of the refrigerator. It's warm. He

bangs the side of the refrigerator to get it to work.

FRANKIE: Shoot...

> *(FRANKIE slams the refrigerator door*
> *shut and goes back inside the trailer. We*
> *hear some rough openings and closing of*
> *drawers and cupboard doors and muffled*
> *profanities. After a moment or two he*
> *appears with a screwdriver and starts*
> *to work on the back of the refrigerator.*
> *During this, SHYANNE enters, unnoticed*
> *by FRANKIE, wearing her shades – she's*
> *in a bad way.)*

Hey, Shy, we gotta do something about this

cooler! It's gone again. I seen one in

Chuck's Fleamart for twenty bucks...

(He stares at Shyanne)

Whoa! What the fuck? Shy?

SHYANNE: Not now, Frankie.

FRANKIE: Jeez! Come here, come here, sit down.

SHYANNE: Don't! Just... don't make a scene, ok?

She squats on a crate.

FRANKIE: What you get up to last night...?

SHYANNE holds her head in her hands and shakes her head.

SHYANNE: Beat it, Frankie! I'm only just down to a seven from a ten. Jesus! I'm such a jerk!! What was I thinking!

FRANKIE tenderly removes SHYANNE's shades.

FRANKIE: Oh my God... Shy... Shy, what happened to you?

SHYANNE: ...I took a ride. With a customer.

FRANKIE: Why? You're the one always telling the girls don't take risks...

SHYANNA: Think I'm some kinda pass around pussy?

FRANKIE: No. I ain't ever seen you like this.

SHYANNE: Well, get a good look kid, 'cos it's the last time, ok? 'Cos I'm gonna quit this game

soon enough. Jesus Christ, all that bending
over backwards, squatting night after night
on low hopes and high heels, I'm ageing
in dog years, Frankie, and the customers,
they see it in me. And so does Melvin.

FRANKIE: Why take a ride? I don't get it.

SHYANNE: Think I haven't asked myself a hundred times
already, why did I take a ride with a customer?
Why. The. Fuck? I got the cloud on it now.
But last night, some guy got the better of me.
I'm always one step ahead of the crazies, I see
'em coming. But psychos, ha! They run faster
than me. And I am so tired, Frankie, dog tired.
Last night, when this dick shit was pawing
at me with a blade in one hand and his cock
in the other, that's when the psycho tricked
me into trusting him. Guess I am stupid.

FRANKIE: What did the cops say?

SHYANNE: The who?

FRANKIE: You went to the cops, right?

SHYANNE: Hello? You seen the color of my skin, lately?

FRANKIE: Erm???

SHYANNE: You any idea know how many times I get

pulled over for a 'speeding ticket', or "is

this your ve-hicle lady?" or any excuse

for a pat down while the white trash fly

past me at hundred miles an hour?

FRANKIE: What about the guy?

SHYANNE: Oh, you mean the nice white motherfuckin'

psycho who came to my rescue? The guy with

the Hollywood smile? The one who then beat

the shit outta me "you half human house

nigger" 'cos he thought I'd ghost ride him

for free in the back seat of his car? Oh, yeah,

they banged him up. What do you think?

He got away with it, just like they always

do! If I think about it, I might just explode

'cos right now, I've reached ten going over

and over like this and them clouds are fit to

burst. So, shut up will you and let me relax.

FRANKIE: You okay, Shyanne?

SHYANNE: Urrrgh!... I'm just letting off a head of steam,

ok? These last 12 month, I've been getting

mixed messages from my angel cards. I'm

all discombobulated. Momma Moonshine needs some voodoo time - alone.

FRANKIE: I got this magic trick I can do for you if you let me...

SHYANNE: Are you shitting me?

FRANKIE, softly whistling the ET theme, puts an 'ET finger' to SHYANNE's temple in slow motion, presses gently and releases.

FRANKIE: You all better now?

SHYANNE: I dunno.

FRANKIE: You're so... pretty.

SHYANNE: I ain't feelin' pretty.

(FRANKIE sighs heavily. SHYANNE realizes something is wrong.)

Why ain't you at work?

FRANKIE: ... Alvin's gonna fire me, I know he is. We had a run in last night on the phone, told me not to show up for my shift today.

SHYANNE: Why?

FRANKIE: Some jerk, a customer. He was pretty mean to me. Threatened me with all kinds of violence. I gave back as good I got.

SHYANNE: You toss a scaldin' hot pot of coffee on his
            head?

FRANKIE: I wish. I yelled right back at him. And guess
            what? Seems like him and Alvin go back
            a long way. Alvin wants me to apologize,
            I told him no, so he told me not to show
            up. And then he yelled, "there's gonna be
            a few big changes from now on, he-she".

Pause.

SHYANNE: "She-ape". Those were the psycho's last words
            to me. "I'll whip yo ass and tame you, put you in
            a cage, you fuckin' no-good for nuttin' she-ape."

FRANKIE: No way!

SHYANNE: … I can't take much more, Frankie.

FRANKIE: I can't take Alvin, "he-she", "freak" all the time.

SHYANNE: Look, I know I'm still trying to get my head
            round a lot of the fucked up things you say.
            But one thing you're not, and that's a freak.

FRANKIE: Why don't Alvin see it that way?

SHYANNE: 'Cos he's Alvin. And maybe for him it's
            like…like…

FRANKIE: What? Like what?

SHYANNE: ... Like when two different species meet.

FRANKIE: Erm...

SHYANNE: You know, like what would a... cat, yeah a cat, what would a cat do if it met a whale for the first time, huh? Know what I'm saying?

FRANKIE: No.

SHYANNE: You know, like the cat feels pretty normal and sure, it's met a few dogs and mice along the way. But to the cat, this ain't terrifying. Until it sees a whale for the first time and thinks to itself "Shit the fuck, Jesus Christ! Check out that motherfuckin' freak! It's a million fucking times bigger than me!" But to the whale, that's all pretty normal. He don't give a shit what he looks like or how big he is. He don't give a shit what the cat thinks. 'Cos he's bigger than that.

FRANKIE: You saying I'm like a cat or a whale?

SHYANNE: No, numbskull. I'm just saying, be more whale about it. Stand up for yourself, give out.

Frankie cuddles into Shyanne

SCENE 9

The following day.

SHYANNE: Alvin's gonna fire you?

FRANKIE: Him and "he-she whales" don't mix. If I wanna be a guy at the diner, he's gonna fire me, and by all accounts, he's got every right to do so. Or, I could agree to his new conditions.

SHYANNE: New conditions?

FRANKIE: He's gonna make me sign a contract tomorrow morning before I start my shift.

ALVIN: Take it, or leave it, stick dick... Of course, we could always come to an arrangement.

FRANKIE: What kinda arrangement?

ALVIN: To continuing your employment.

FRANKIE: I'd really appreciate that, Alvin.

ALVIN: On one condition.

FRANKIE: What?

ALVIN comes in close to FRANKIE and lays a hand on his chest and massages his breast, slowly. FRANKIE freezes.

ALVIN: I'm told your freezer's got a top shelf, fully stacked.

(FRANKIE *tries to move away, but*
ALVIN restrains him, firmly, but
gently, moving one hand down towards
FRANKIE'S *crotch.*)

And you got yourself a bald pink taco in the
underground car lot.

FRANKIE: I, I, I'm not finding this a comfortable
situation.

ALVIN: I'm a reasonable kinda guy, you're a good
little food server, I'll give you that. But the
customers, they swine, they know what they
like and don't like. And this swine of mine, hell,
they're tellin' me they all gonna got fed up with
me dishing up their grits and pancakes with
a dash of freak on the side, especially when
it snaps back. Maybe the answer is, we all
should try get to know you, just a little better.

FRANKIE: Erm…

ALVIN: Want me to S.P.L it out for you? You still got
all the goods God gave you, so who cares
if you wear long pants and tie your titties
up in knots? And maybe that's something

that's missing from my menu, my late nite

special menu, for my special folk. You go

right ahead, be a daytime dude with the

hash browns, I don't care. But in return, on

Tuesdays, you'll be servin' up all kinda sweet

things on that dish of yours in Motel 6.

FRANKIE: No way!

ALVIN: You been a cooch potato for too long, bet

you're a real Pamela Anderson between

the sheets when you get going.

FRANKIE: No! No! I won't do it!

ALVIN: See anyone else lining up to take you on,

he-she? Only Alvin.

FRANKIE: Are you for real? Is that the only way I

keep my job?

ALVIN: Unless you do the pink number, the whole

nine yards and no more he-she shit. Non-

negotiable, kid. Sign, keep your job,

your modesty in your fanny pack and I

guarantee, you won't interest me, or no-

one else, for that matter, not in pink.

FRANKIE: *(to Shyanne)*

So that's it. If I wanna keep my job, I'm gonna

have to sign this contract of his. Or worse.

SHYANNE: He needs reporting to the authorities!

FRANKIE: What's the point? No one cares. If I don't do

exactly what he says, he's gonna fire me

and I ain't ever gonna start on the T.

SHYANNE cuddles into FRANKIE.

SHYANNE: Prick.

FRANKIE: Prick.

SCENE 10

SHYANNE: The day momma dragged me to the trailer park,

I nearly died. She packed a suitcase, bought

two tickets for the Greyhound and seven hours

later, I was in a place I didn't recognize, a world

that wasn't mine. I'd just turned ten, I guess - I

don't recall. She told me the only thing I was

putting in my belly for the next month was lima

beans - 'cos we had no money. We was f-l-a-t

broke. My new world was a trailer. In a run-

down shit heap. No running water, no facilities,

if you will. I told myself, when I grow up, I'd
never not have enough money. One day I'd be
like one of them princesses I used to watch
on the TV with my daddy. But daddy, well,
he disappeared. Vanished into thin air. Ain't
never seen him again. Could be dead for all I
know... I musta been going on for... twelve, I
don't know, I got the cloud on this, but maybe
I was in sixth grade, when I noticed something
different about my momma. Came home
from school one day and she was laughing.
Laughing! Turns out she'd got it on with one of
the maintaining men. Ugly looking skunk, bad
breath, never seemed to bathe. Always riding
around on that little clapped out golf cart thing,
steering it with is knees, drinking beer in one
hand and when he caught my eye, his cock
in the other. Never did see him fix anything.
One night, he crawled under a trailer, drunk,
to get out of the rain and got electrocuted
from faulty wiring. He must a got lucky - he
lived. Long enough to be waiting for me on

the porch when my breasts began to show. Old
enough to know that two fingers of his stuck
up my vagina was definitely not a good thing.

SCENE 11

*Frankie is revealed dressed as a waitress in a pink
uniform dress, open white shirt and wearing a cap with
a pony tail attached to it. He looks at himself in a mirror
and wails loudly.*

SCENE 12

SHYANNE: After a year of him fingering me in the dark
and putting his cheap bourbon stained breath on
my lips, I told myself "enough is enough" and I
plucked up the courage to tell my momma. She
looked at me, her eyes getting wider and with a
sweat breaking out on her skin. She slapped me so
hard across the face, I fell backwards and cracked
my head against the stove. Spent the night in the
ER, wishing it was the morgue. But a kindly nurse

took pity on me as I lay in my hospital bed. One
night she whispered into my childlike ear, words
I'll never forget. A few days later I came home to
group of Jamaican drug dealers hanging around
the trailer with my momma - and he was gone.
Don't know what happened to him, but took
an educated guess and gave myself a straight A
for intuition. I just smiled to myself, imagining.
And that felt good. It didn't last forever, mind.
By the time I was fifteen, I was already in my
prime and... but that's another story. At sixteen, I
dated Patrick, a crack dealer for six, seven months,
maybe more. He was kind to me, introduced me
to coke, kept me supplied in regular percs that
made the world seem like it was an okay place
after all. One time, he took me to an agent, we
went to a club, got talking to the boss - who got
me drunk - and after that I took off all my clothes
and found I had a natural gift for dancing in the
nude. And for that I could take home two to
three hundred dollars a night. I didn't never go
back to school from that day on and I ain't seen

my momma since. The men folk of the county
were my educators now. Know what I'm saying?

*FRANKIE is scrubbing the ponytail attached to the cap
from his diner uniform in a bucket.*

FRANKIE: I love that story.

SHYANNE: Ain't a story, hun.

> *(A beat)*

> ... Will you do my legs?

> > *(SHYANNE stretches her legs and waggles
them. FRANKIE stops what he's doing
with the pan and quite naturally kneels in
front of SHYANNE. He begins to unzip
Shyanne's boots and slides them off and
rubs her legs. SHYANNE is transported.)*

> Aww, baby, that's good. I swear I never
met no guy with hands like yours.

FRANKIE is rubbing SHYANNE's calf.

FRANKIE: You got a furnace going on here.

SHYANNE: What you expect? These are my twins,
Lionel and Ritchie and I'm on 'em

> *(Sings)*

> "All night long".

(Sighs)

Baby, I gotta let my twinkle toes breathe
for a few minutes. Shit, even smiling all
night makes my fucking head ache.

FRANKIE: Was it a good night? You know, dollar wise.

SHYANNE: Uh-huh.

FRANKIE: How much?

SHYANNE: I have no idea. You count it if you want.
I trust you.

*SHYANNE pulls out a fistful of notes from her top. She
lets them drop to the ground. FRANKIE scrapes them
into a bundle, quickly counts.*

FRANKIE: Jeez! Shyanne, couple a hundred, maybe more.

SHYANNE: Thank you, Lionel and Ritchie!

(Sings)

"All night long"……

(Suddenly tender, intense)

I want you take it. All of it. Go on.

FRANKIE: Why? I don't under(stand) -

SHYANNE: Just take it, kid, do as I say. Don't make me
triggy saying "no". Reckon you need it more than
I do. Go get yourself a shot of that 'no shit' T.

FRANKIE: Shy, I don't know what to... I mean, I ain't
even seen a medic or nuttin'.

SHYANNE: One of my regulars, get this, dick the size
of a long-tailed weasel, knows this other guy,
supplies him with his 'male enhancements',
know what I mean, on the other side of
town. He'll start you off. Reckon we got
enough here for one nut, at least.

*(FRANKIE tips the boots upside down
and a few more bills drop to the floor.
FRANKIE looks at SHYANNE with a
"what the fuck?!" face.)*

You miss your momma?

FRANKIE: I don't wanna talk about her. She don't ever
talk about me, except maybe to God.
And then only on Sundays.

SHYANNE: When I was a kid, I hated Sundays.

FRANKIE: Why?

SHYANNE: The so-called Reverend Raymond Goodman,
that's why.

*GOODMAN is working his hands up SHYANNE's legs,
leering.*

GOODMAN: Don't you be afraid, sweetie, this is the

Lord's work, he's gonna fill your soul

with his Almighty goodness. He's chosen

you, so say nuttin' to anyone else about

this, we don't want them envyin' your

special status now, do we? Promise?"

SHYANNE: And then he fucked me.

A moment of silence.

FRANKIE: My grandpa was always very kind to me.

Deep down inside, I think he got me.

GRANDPA runs his hands gently through FRANCE'S hair.

GRANDPA: You're perfect, just the way you are.

FRANKIE: I prayed very night he could be my daddy.

I guess God ran outta miracles.

GRANDPA: I'm not be long for this earth, son. I'll

always be by your side. You have my

take down rifle when I'm gone.

FRANKIE: Daddy was dead set against it.

DADDY: No way! Guns ain't for girls!

FRANKIE: He hung it on the mantle, on two rusty nails

to taunt me. I hated him for that.

A moment.

SHYANNE: You know, when I told my momma about
the Minister, she… she went right
on ahead and she beat me!

MOMMA: Breathe a word of that again, I'm gonna hang
you up from a tree, you get me'? You get me?!
Now pull on your stockings, put your best shoes
on and get yourself to church. Momma's got busy
to be. I don't wanna see your ugly face before five.

SHYANNE: And he'd be waitin'. Just remembering his
jambalaya breath on me sends me to a ten!

*(Irritated, pulling her arm sharply away
from FRANKIE)*

Can you get back to my feet?

*(FRANKIE nods and moves back to
SHYANNE'S feet.)*

Mmm… That's soooo good…

(SHYANNE indicates she needs another beer.)

Did I ever tell you…?

FRANKIE: What?

SHYANNE: I coulda had a screen test?

FRANKIE: No shit? When?

SHYANNE: I don't know, it's kinda cloudy.

FRANKIE: How? I mean, what for?

SHYANNE: As a body double.

FRANKIE: No shit. A body double? Who?

SHYANNE: Go on - guess.

FRANKIE: Er, er...

SHYANNE: C'mon, take a wild guess!

FRANKIE: Whoopi?

SHYANNE: Jeez, Frankie!

FRANKIE: Er... the one from Star Trek? The one with

her finger in her ear all the time?

(SHYANNE looks like she'll explode.)

Sorry. Whitney? Yeah, Whitney?

SHYANNE: Yeah, yeah, that woulda been good...Oh

come on, Frankie, think, think!... Ok, ok,

I'll spill, Geena Davis! Geena fucking

Davis! Can you believe that?

FRANKIE can't believe it.

FRANKIE: Geena Davis!?

SHYANNE: Can you believe that?

FRANKIE: Er...

SHYANNE: Back in the day, in a light flesh tone body

suit, big red hairpiece, I was a dead ringer

- from behind. That coulda been me in
that Thunderbird convertible heading
for oblivion into the Grand Can-yon!
Yee-ha!

FRANKIE: So, what happened?

SHYANNE: She and Susan Sarandon drove right over
the edge so's they wouldn't get caught.

FRANKIE: I knows that.

SHYANNE: It was free-dom.

FRANKIE: Yeah, I knows that. What happened to you?
Did you get the job?

SHYANNE: *(her mood darkens)*

That's another story.

FRANKIE: You can't leave me hanging.

SHYANNE: Don't push me, okay? Like I said...

FRANKIE: I guess... Such a once in a life(time)...

SHYANNE: I said, zip it! I don't wanna talk about it no
more. Get off me.

Pause.

FRANKIE: ... screen double, huh? Sure beats being a food
server in a pink dress. Hey! Reckon
I could be a screen double?

SHYANNE: *(extremely patronising and hurtful)*

Yeah, you and King Kong. No, no, how about

Godzilla! Yeah, yeah, that's about it.

(SHYANNE laughs cruelly at her own

joke. The severity of this hits FRANKIE.

He pulls away.)

Or there's the donkey, you know, the one

from Shrek! You could be bishreksual, yeah!

FRANKIE: Just forget it, Shyanne.

SHYANNE: You gotta similar kinda swagger and you're

always cracking jokes, 'cept they ain't funny.

FRANKIE: Just drop it, huh?

SHYANNE pulls herself up in surprise, she realizes she

gone too far.

SHYANNE: Kid, I'm only messing.

FRANKIE: Sure. Like everyone else, just like Alvin.

"He-she", "tranny-be", "freak",

"stick dick", you name it.

SHYANNE: Get a grip! It's only a joke. J.O.A.K. Ha ha

ha. Lighten up.

FRANKIE: You supposed to be my friend! You know I

hate that pink number, I can't even

look at myself. What's the point of

me? What's the point of us?

SHYANNE: So messy.

FRANKIE: Think you're better than me? You ain't. 'Cos

we're cut from the same grain. Below

ground. Truth is, "Amethyst, Momma

Moonshine, Shyanne", you're just as

messy, and that makes you a fake.

SHYANNE: Fake? We talking motherfuckin' fake here?

'Cos if so, open your eyes and take a l-o-n-g good

look at yourself in that invisible glass, Frankie.

Tell me what you see. No? Ok, I'll tell you. Some

washed up guy with no romantic lead, 'cos you

can't even love yourself. Me? I'm all woman.

FRANKIE: Yeah, all woman, yeah, who opens her legs for

every guy who stuffs a dollar down

her top. All woman, yeah.

SHYANNE: All woman, yeah, all woman, and you listen

up and listen good. I know what it feels like to

be all woman, 'cos one time I gave birth to a

beautiful little princess! And I didn't even know

I was pregnant! I was fifteen, for fuck's sake!

FRANKIE: You ain't never told me you had... a kid.

SHYANNE: There's a lot I don't tell you, kid.

> *(Laughs, bitterly)*
>
> Funny, you'd be about the same age, I guess. You know, I called that beautiful baby "Rochelle".
>
> *(Suddenly angry)*
>
> And they go call her "Andrea". Imagine that! "Andrea"! What kind of name is that for a woman of color, huh? "Andrea". "Andrea". No. I don't get it... And I been told recently she's gonna be a medic. A medic, Frankie. With a specialty in functional incontinence. What the fuck? She's got brains, Frankie, motherfuckin' brains, not like her lame assed motherfuckin' retard proper momma. She's using brains to pay her bills. That kid has a future stretching w-a-y ahead of her I could never give - and I'll tell you something for nuttin', she's still the sunrise to my sunset, the stars to my moon, and just 'cos I didn't have the facilities, the facilities if you will, mind, at the time to take care of her, just 'cos she didn't have the poppa, the poppa, mind, to share all

them TV princess ways, don't mean nuttin' and don't mean that my beautiful baby Rochelle isn't in my heart every single minute of the day.

FRANKIE: You keep so much in. I don't get it. How come this is the first time I get to hear about her? I tell you everything.

SHYANNE: *(reaching ten)*

Do I ask? No. But you - you just can't help spilling all them bitter beans you got stored up inside you. And right now, you're dragging me down with all your lame assed messy self-pity, yeah, that and your negativity. You're King of negativity!

FRANKIE: I ain't, Shy, I ain't, I promise, I swear on my grandpa's gun, I ain't that person. And if I am, I can change, I'm gonna change, I promise. That's the truth. Where you going?

SHYANNE: Dead momma walking. Outta my way, boy, you got me all worked up to a ten!

FRANKIE: Yeah? Yeah? Well, maybe I won't be here you when get back.

SHYANNE: So, so eye cry, hoo-hoo-boo.

FRANKIE: I mean it. Dead or alive.

SHYANNE: Know what? I'm so damned triggy right now,

I ain't got no time for this. Yours is the

last mixed up face I wanna see written

all over with your snowflake pity. Truth?

You're just a nobody tryin' to be a nobody.

And that's the motherfuckin' truth.

FRANKIE is destroyed.

SCENE 13

Later.

The sound of crickets. SHYANNE, half asleep.

FRANKIE cradles her head and strokes it.

SHYANNE: I'm sorry.....

FRANKIE: I know.

(SHYANNE falls asleep)

"Sorry". Shyanne you ain't got nuttin' to be sorry

for, it ain't your fault. It's me. You been nuttin' but

kind in taking me in off the street like you did,

when you didn't have to. I still ain't a hundred

percent certain why you'd do such a crazy thing

like that, you crazy bitch. That means a lot to

me. 'Cos to everyone else, I'm a freak. I still can't get used to folk calling me those names. I guess I bring out the worst in them. I know I'm a real big disappointment to my daddy and he hates the way I turned out. But I sure wasn't gonna let him and the Bible drive me to take my own life, though sometimes it felt like the only way for me, especially after them conversion courses the Pastor made me attend. There was nuttin' in these 'cures' that simply said, "you're OK, it'll be OK, don't worry, it's OK". 'Cos it wasn't OK. It wasn't a phase, and nobody was the slightest bit sorry what they put me through. "Sorry". It's like a word invented in a foreign language, kinda Frenchy. "Sorry". Sorry for bringing me into this wide world, sorry for the miracle of my life, sorry for the yellings off my daddy, like if I screwed up for no kind of reason. There was always a reason, some truth buried deep down in a bible reading. And he were never sorry. He beat me so many times, made me stand out in the rain and the cold, made me lie down with the animals at night - I ain't talking no comfy stable here with all that nice, warm straw you read about in the New Testament, no. He always found a reason, even if he had to dig out his eye glasses to find it. 'Cos in my daddy's head, he didn't need no reason to pick on me, no matter how small that reason was, no matter how small I was, no matter how small I was feelin' at the time. Maybe I still feel small? Maybe I am small? Maybe I'm in my comfort zone. A small comfort zone. 'Cos I ain't ever done big. No big hopes, no big dreams, no big money, no big dog. I'm especially pissed when it comes to the big dog. But hey, no big deal. I just wish my folks could meet you, take you to their hearts like I've to mine. 'Cos I know you'll never leave me. And I'll never leave your side so long as you want me. Me being a boy would be the least of their concerns! Who's sorry now? Not me. 'Cos, truth told, I ain't the sorrying kind, I ain't got a sorry face, I ain't got a sorry hide, I ain't got a sorry nuttin'. So what's left to feel sorry for?! Nuttin'. And I ain't about to start apologizin', now. Sorry.

ACT TWO

SCENE 14

A few months later.

*SHYANNE appears in ecstasy. She is crouching. As the
light becomes stronger, she reaches her hands up towards
it. It's clear she is revering a very small object (a calling
card) in her hand. She slowly begins to stand and the
morning daylight fills the stage and she dances, her eyes
on the business card all the time as if it were a guy, a guy
with money. FRANKIE, returning from her breakfast
shift stops short and watches SHYANNE, shiftily.*

SHYANNE: Yeah, sweetie - can I call you that?... Y'know,
I don't talk to all the hogs we get in here.
And I never bothered to learn grunt, know
what I'm saying? You got the face of an angel.
And the voice of a sweet, sweet bee. You have
me buzzing with your soft zee sweet talking,
making nectar in my ears... Sure, I'm open

to all kinds of offers, reasonable don't come into it... I knew that from the moment I laid my eyes on you... I like your style... some would say, pizazz-zee-zee-zee. You pizazz-zee-zee a good judge of character, I can tell and a respectable man, like yourself, deserves tremendous respect. Guys like you just make me wanna rejazzle my dazzle, all over.

(She kisses the calling card)

I think we're all gonna have a very close working relationship, know what I'm saying? But that does depends on the size of your deposit. Think of my lips like an ATM. 'Cept the money goes the other way, of course.

(SHYANNE is turning on the spot, elated, her eyes closed. When she stops, she sees FRANKIE and is startled.)

Frankie! I ain't gonna tell you again, quit looking at me like that. Creeps me out, baby!

FRANKIE: What's that in your hand?

SHYANNE: Oh... that's nuttin'. Just one of my angel cards, I musta mislaid it, and there it was, like...

FRANKIE: Don't lie to me. I don't keep secrets from you.

SHYANNE: Maybe I don't wanna know what's in your

closet. Maybe you don't wanna

know what's in my hand.

FRANKIE: Why you being like this?

SHYANNE: Like what?

FRANKIE: This. Have I offended you in some way?

SHYANNE: Why would you say that?

FRANKIE: 'Cos, you looked... happy, before. I ain't seen

you this happy in a long while.

SHYANNE: Is that so?

FRANKIE: Why you so happy?

SHYANNE: Jer, jer, jer, happy, happy, happy... there, I

said it three times, I must be really happy!

Happy, now? Even know what happy is, kid?

(FRANKIE hangs his head.)

Aww, c'mon... not that, not the head, you

know I can't take the head bit... I ain't

saying sorry, no, sir, I ain't got nuttin' to be

sorry for. Huh? Hey? Kid? Talk to me.

(FRANKIE squats on a crate, his head in

his hands.)

Aww, fuck you Frankie, that ain't

fair! You know that ain't fair.

FRANKIE: I got nuttin' to say.

SHYANNE: Fine. Fine, maybe you're right, maybe I am

happy. For once. There, I fessed up. Happy?

Happy. Happy, happy, happy, happy, happy,

happy. And I *have* got something to tell you.

FRANKIE: Is it a guy?

SHYANNE: No. Yes.

FRANKIE: I knew it!

SHYANNE: And you gonna be happy for me, too.

FRANKIE: I am?

SHYANNE: Yes - 'cos I got me a job.

FRANKIE: Y'already gotta job.

SHYANNE: A new job.

FRANKIE: What new job?

SHYANNE: A job that's new, for fuck's sake, that kinda

job.

FRANKIE: What's the job?

SHYANNE: Kinda like my current job.

FRANKIE: A dancing job?

SHYANNE: More like, entertainment.

FRANKIE: Y'already entertain folk.

SHYANNE: Not these folk.

FRANKIE: What folk?

SHYANNE: Folk with money.

FRANKIE: Folk already give you money.

SHYANNE: Not this kinda money.

FRANKIE: What kinda money?

SHYANNE: Money that'll buy me things.

FRANKIE: What kinda things?

SHYANNE: Things I only ever dreamed of.

FRANKIE: What kinda dreams?

SHYANNE: Day dreams, Frankie, day dreams. I'm sick
of workin' my ass at night to pay the bills.

FRANKIE: ... This new job?

SHYANNE: Uh-huh?

FRANKIE: Is it round here?

SHYANNE: Not round here, that's for sure.

FRANKIE: Where, then?

SHYANNE: Where I wanna be.

FRANKIE: Where's that?

SHYANNE: I'm a little cloudy on the detail. I need to
establish the facts.

FRANKIE: When?

SHYANNE: When I have my next meeting.

FRANKIE: When's that then?

SHYANNE: When he calls me.

FRANKIE: When who calls you?

SHYANNE: The guy.

FRANKIE: The guy? What guy?

SHYANNE: The guy who gave me this.

SHYANNE waves the business card.

FRANKIE: What *is* that?

SHYANNE: What's this?

FRANKIE: Yeah, what's that?

SHYANNE: This is only a goddam calling card, Frankie!

I ain't ever been given no goddam calling

card, not like this, printed on premium card.

FRANKIE: Can I see it?

(SHYANNE shows it at arm's length –

FRANKIE leans in to read.)

So, who's Anthony H. Fro...frull...?

SHYANNE: Fröehlich. Like it says. Entrepreneur.

FRANKIE: What does he entrepreneur in?

SHYANNE: Hello - I'm in the leezure trade. So's he.

> Talent spots talent, even in gynecology
>
> row. He owns a club.

FRANKIE: What club?

SHYANNE: Precious Stones.

FRANKIE: Where?

SHYANNE: Where? Vegas, of course!

FRANKIE: Vegas?

SHYANNE: Uh-huh, Las Vegas.

FRANKIE: Precious Stones, huh?

SHYANNE: Yeah. Or, maybe Little Gems... I can't quite
recall, I still got the cloud, like I says, on
account of all the motherfuckin' excitement.

FRANKIE: Never heard of none of 'em. Not in Vegas.

SHYANNE: You ever been to Vegas?

FRANKIE: Nope. Never been to Vegas.

SHYANNE: Well how in God's name would you know
what's not and what's what in Vegas
if you ain't never been to Vegas?

FRANKIE: I saw "Leaving Las Vegas" at the movies.

SHYANNE: Er, jer-jer-jer-jer... I'm *going* to Las Vegas,
baby. My guess is you know nuttin' about
Vegas, and "Leaving Las Vegas", well, that's just

made up Vegas and best left behind Vegas.

FRANKIE: I know there's a Crazy Horse.

SHYANNE: Crazy Horse? Some kinda relation of yours?

FRANKIE: No! The guys at the diner were talking about it one day.

SHYANNE: What do they know? They at this movie, too, cracking their teeth on their beer nuts?

FRANKIE: … When you gonna start this new job?

SHYANNE: As soon as I sign the contract.

FRANKIE: You gotta a contract?

SHYANNE: I ain't got the contract yet, but when I do, I'm gonna sign the contract.

FRANKIE: When?

SHYANNE: Er, jer, jer, jer, when I've read the goddam contract. Think I'm retarded? Couple of days' time. I've got me a meeting all lined up.

FRANKIE: A meeting?

SHYANNE: A meeting. To collect the contract, of course, so I can read the contract, numbskull.

FRANKIE: Oh.

SHYANNE: Oh?

FRANKIE: It's OK. Nuttin'.

SHYANNE: Oh no, no you don't. Since when has "oh" never been nuttin' with you?

FRANKIE: Momma Moonshine, Shyanne - you gotta do what you gotta do.

SHYANNE: That's my intention.

FRANKIE: 'cept....

SHYANNE: 'cept what?

FRANKIE: Where does this all leave me?

SHYANNE turns away to think on her feet.

SHYANNE: I ain't going nowhere without you, kid. Nowhere. We gotta stick together, like two scooters under the same shell. I know! Come with me. To Vegas.

FRANKIE: Vegas?

SHYANNE: Vegas. Think about it, Frankie!

(FRANKIE stares, unable to take this in.)

Say something, will you?

FRANKIE: Vegas? Me? Vegas?

SHYANNE: Yeah. Let's go make some trouble.

FRANKIE: I don't know what to say. That's just the nicest thing anyone's ever gonna and done for me. I mean... whoa! 'Cos when I get to Vegas, I'm gonna get me a proper job where I won't have to wear a stupid pink dress and I can train.

SHYANNE: Train?

FRANKIE: As a mechanic - daddy was always dead against that.

DADDY: No way! Girls don't fix cars!

FRANKIE: I'm gonna be the best. I'm gonna be the one in demand. They're all gonna be bringing their ve-hicles to my yard to be fixed and I'll be the one looking down the lens calling the shots, taking their blue collar dollars. And when those big bucks start rolling in, first thing I'm gonna do is find a medic, lay my hands on some T and I'm gonna change. I'm gonna be the guy I was born to be.

SHYANNE: Good man!

FRANKIE: And then I'm gonna buy us the biggest SUV money can buy.

SHYANNE: Hell, yeah, a real big motherfucker.

FRANKIE: Yeah! And on Labor Day we'll drive out to the Grand Canyon, take a picnic, pack some beers in the cooler and watch the eagles, gliding on them thermals. And then, then…

SHYANNE: Yeah, what? What, then?

FRANKIE: ... We'll get a boat.

SHYANNE: Shit. I can't swim.

FRANKIE: I don't care, 'cos we're gonna sail, right across
           Lake Mead, get dead center, switch off the
           engines, and on days like this, we're gonna lie
           back on the deck like millionaires until the
           night time take us. I don't mean nuttin' queer
           by that. And in the morning, we'll make for
           the shore, climb aboard our awesome SUV and
           head straight on, back to the Strip, for an all
           you can eat breakfast buffet at Circus Circus.

SHYANNE: Circus Circus - OK, I can live with that...

FRANKIE: See, I had an aunt once, Bertha Anna-Marie,
           she went to Circus Circus and won five
           hundred bucks on the Lone Wolf slots
           with her first nickel. Straight up.

SHYANNE: Good for her. Did she stay lucky?

FRANKIE: Nope. Got mown down on the Strip by a
           pedophile on the run in a stolen stretch limo,
           broke her back and both her legs. Worst of all,
           lost the use of the arm she played the slots with.

SHYANNE: Er, jer-jer-jer-jer! What about the other arm?

FRANKIE: Used it to slit her wrists in a bath tub brim
full of vodka she bought with her winnings.

SHYANNE: What happened to the guy?

FRANKIE: Gassed.

> (*They both picture the images in their heads
> for a moment.*)

We'll get a dog.

SHYANNE: What kinda dog?

FRANKIE: A big dog. One of them trained as a Seeing
Eye dog in the event of one of us going
tragically blind. Like my cousin, Cain.

SHYANNE: No shit! You have a cousin who's blind?

FRANKIE: Wasn't always blind. He had this strange
habit. Kept eyeballing the sun without
the use of shades, hours at a time. In the
end, his retina's couldn't take no more.

SHYANNE: Well, kid, that's good, ain't it?

FRANKIE: Why would that be good?

SHYANNE: 'Cos it ain't a medical condition that runs
through the family, know what I'm saying?

FRANKIE: I wouldn't know. He was adopted.

They both picture the images in their heads for a moment.

SHYANNE: Well, you can just go right ahead and get
yourself any old type of dog you want. 'Cos
we're all gonna have a motherfuckin' real
nice home, with land, lots of it, and
horses, somewhere in the desert.

FRANKIE: Somewhere my folks can come visit?

SHYANNE: Er, jer-jer-jer-jer, you seriously gonna ask
that bunch of fucked up weirdos to Vegas?

FRANKIE: Uh-huh, sure, so mom can see the spot where
my aunt Bertha Anna-Marie, the one
struck down by the pedophile -

SHYANNE: Yeah, I knows that.

FRANKIE: Mom ain't ever had closure. It's eating her
alive.

SHYANNE: Well, mmm-mmm-mmm. Ain't you just the
perfect... whatever, all of a sudden? Are you
shitting me?! She gonna get the guided
tour to her own sister's misery? Jeez! What
is it with you, Frankie? I'm offering you a
motherfuckin' way out here and you're throwing
it right back in my face. I don't get it!

FRANKIE: Well, I'm real sorry you feel that way, Shy.

But this is my way out and after my folks tried all that healin' shit thing with me at church, I need to show 'em - I. For. Give. Them. I want them to see me as I really am. Not the little farm girl Barbie with her hair tied up in ribbons. No. That was sad me. This is happy me. Yes. Happy. Happy. Happy. See? I said it three times. The Gospel according to Happy! A testament that God works miracles.

(SHYANNE looks at FRANKIE archly.
They both burst into peals of laughter and
clink bottles.)

Frankie's done with Frances. It's gonna be you, me the new and Las Vegas! That's if you still want me to...

SHYANNE: Sure, sure... It'll figure, ok? Trust me. Have I ever let you down? No. Right now, I gotta pack a bag.

FRANKIE: Why? Where you going?

SHYANNE: That's a stupid question! I've got me some new voodoo matters to consult. This is it, Frankie! The angel cards, they been good

to me. But I'm gonna be extra precautious
this time. This is my way out, too.

FRANKIE: When you coming back?

SHYANNE: When the magic's all mine! That's when!

SHYANNE exits.

SCENE 15

Frankie can't stop himself from dancing with joy.

FRANKIE: Woo-hoo! The last maple syrup surprise is
gonna leave my hands, forever! I'm swapping
chicken grease for axle grease from now on. No
more hash browns, no more sausage links, no
eggs over easy, no bacon strips. No grits. No
English muffins and buttered toast. And no
more coffee, coffee, coffee. Fuck you, sir, and fuck
you ma'am with your fat lips and droopy eyes of
disdain. So if you wanna sit right there and judge
me with those big moon faces of yours waiting
on your Pig Out Platter, followed by your key
lime pies, I got news, good news for y'all. Think
I'm broken? Well, you're broken, too. 'Cos God

made me in his own image, just like you. And
I know that's a bit of head fuck for you, ma'am,
sir, 'cos y'all can't square your own prejudice
and downright hatred with His words of love.
'Cos I now know for sure, He did not make a
mistake when He made me. Y'all the ones makin'
mistakes. Oh, and by the way. You. Ain't. Got. It.
Y'all won't have a nice day now, y'all have a crap
one. Frankie's most definitely going to Vegas
and I'm pretty damn sure, Alvin's goin' to hell.
I got nothing to lose! Las Vegas, here I come!

SCENE 16

*Las Vegas in a dream. SHYANNE, dressed like a million
dollars, sashays elegantly downstage.*

SHYANNE: Well, hell-o Vegas! I can't hear you. I said,
hell-o Las Vegas! Yew-eeh! That's better!
Welcome, welcome everyone to Shyanne's
Show The World Show! I used to go by the
name of "Amethyst", you know, different kinda
stage, different kinda show. No jackin' off in

the front row, sir, the plush can't take it. Well, before we get started, I gotta tell you, I'm living the dream! Hell yeah, yew-eeh! That's right! Dreams do come true! And I don't even have to finger my own cunt - or anyone else's - on this stage tonight! What's that, sir? No, it ain't that kinda show, I'm just getting used to my new situation, that's all, finding my feet, know what I'm saying? And that's why you gonna fall in love with me and the tricks I'm gonna turn in front you tonight which don't involve my upside down tunnel of love. What's that, sir? You want me to do what? I don't think so. Everyone - Get. A. Load of the low life in row 9 and the filth falling outta his mouth. Can we all get a follow spot on him? Yup. That's him. I can see you're no gentleman 'cos you're in the wrong kinda club, sir. With a dick that size, I'd say kindergarten was the right place for you, what do we say, ladies? That's right, yew-eeh, I'm loving this, every motherfuckin' minute and screw you if I ain't to your liking.

'Cos I got here all by myself. By. My. Self, motherfuckers. I was intended to own this stage, just like my angels cards said. Right now, I wanna introduce you to someone whose been the lost to my found, the jerk to my chicken. So please, all you good folks out there, put your hands together and show some appreciation for the only man in my life who never tried to rape me! My personal assistant - Frankie!

> (FRANKIE, *dressed very smartly appears holding a legal size envelope. He shakes hands with SHYANNE.*)

Handsome looking dude, ain't he? You gonna say "hi" to all these good folk?

FRANKIE: *(bashful)*

Hi y'all.

SHYANNE: Fine looking bunch of motherfuckers, ain't they?

FRANKIE: Yep.

SHYANNE: We've both come a long way, and I don't just mean from Texas. Ain't that so?

FRANKIE: Yep.

SHYANNE: No regrets?

FRANKIE: Nope.

SHYANNE: No looking back?

FRANKIE: Nope.

SHYANNE: No looking back, no looking back.

FRANKIE: Nope. Nope. Except, maybe...

SHYANNE: What? What's that you say, darling? Except, what?

SHYANNE forces a smile.

FRANKIE: Maybe I shoulda had... a baby...? Before,

you know, all this and the like.

SHYANNE: Shoulda what?

FRANKIE: Had a ba(by) -

SHYANNE: Jer-jer-jer-jer, I fucking heard you first time.

What? What. The. Fuck has gotten into

you? That's. So. Messy. You're king mess!

FRANKIE: This came for you.

FRANKIE offers the envelope and exits.

SHYANNE: Gimme that!... It's the contract. This is it,

the contract of my dreams.

(The Las Vegas performer returns. All

smiles. Dreamily, to the audience.)

Vee-va Las Vay-gus, I ain't ever leaving you!

Wonderful dreams do come true! If you
good folk'll excuse me... just one moment...
while I inspect... the finest of... details...

*(SHYANNE starts to reads the paperwork,
rooted to the spot. She turns over the page.
Her face collapses. Shyanne rips at her
dress, fighting back tears. She falls to the
ground.)*

Urrghhh! Urggghhh!! Urgggghhhhhh!!!!!!

*The Las Vegas dream fades away. SHYANNE is in a
heap.*

SCENE 17

Reality. The trailer. The sound of crickets.

SHYANNE: Kansas! It says... Wichita, Kansas!

FRANKIE: Kansas? What about Vegas?

SHYANNE: According to this... piece of motherfuckin'
shit, there is no Vegas.

FRANKIE: You told me, Vegas. What about your voodoo? I thought you had the magic all sewn up.

SHYANNE: Yeah, well shit happens, kid, and the angels,

they musta had an off day. This dog aged dancer is heading for the pound 'cos she just lost her bite and mislaid her bark. You just gotta get Vegas outta you head. OK?

FRANKIE: I can't. Vegas, Vegas, Vegas….

SHYANNE: Stop that.

FRANKIE: Nope. You told me I could have a dog, a big dog, I've been looking at dog chews. What am I gonna tell my folks? Vegas, Vegas, Vegas…

SHYANNE: I said, stop that!

> *(SYHANNE slaps FRANKIE who is stunned into silence.)*

It's Wichita, The Erogenous Zone Club or jack shit. That's what it says. I'm gonna be a low ho on high heels forever. You, you just gotta stick with your tits and your hoo-ha.

FRANKIE: I don't wanna stick with my tits and my hoo-ha, that's the old me, I want the new me.

SHYANNE: Think I wanna be a low ho on high heels?

FRANKIE: It ain't fair.

SHYANNE: Boom-boom, life ain't fair, kid. Not for the likes of us. Get. Used. To. It! Only pork you'll be pulling from now on will be in some low-rent barbecue shack in good old downtown Wichita, Kansas. Shit. And I just got myself fired.

FRANKIE: Fired? When?

SHYANNE: Last night.

FRANKIE: How?

SHYANNE: I gone and told Melvin "you motherfuckin' jackhole, Elvis is back in the buildin', so save your five knuckle shuffle for the jon." No way I'm going to ER to beg!

FRANKIE: He's in the ER? Why?

SHYANNE: 'Cos I threw my cognac on his fly and set fire to it.

FRANKIE: Jeez!

SHYANNE: That's what he said. Kinda screaming, like.

FRANKIE: You're amazing, Shyanne.

SHYANNE: I kinda think so, too. And for once, that felt good.

   They break into laughter.

FRANKIE: What you gonna do, now?

SHYANNE: Oobleeyay my boobleeyay. I've got me a plan.

FRANKIE: What kinda plan?

SHYANNE: A plan that gets us to Vegas!

FRANKIE: How you gonna do that?

SHYANNE: He's gonna change his mind. I swear by all the magic I got in my purse, Mr. Anthony H. Fröehlich, he's gonna be a different man, time I'm finished with him.

FRANKIE: I believe you Shyanne. Go, go, go! There really is something... magic about you tonight.

SHYANNE: I feel it, too. Pack your stuff and be ready to leave when I get back. Things are gonna change, I know it.

FRANKIE: Me, too. Time me and Alvin had words.

SCENE 18.

FRANKIE smartens himself up as he talks and looks his most masculine.

FRANKIE: I knew where Alvin lived, 'cos I read the
overdue notices he brings into the office to hide
from Mrs. Alvin. I'm standing on his porch,
seems like eternity, I almost turn tail. Until I
remember all the bad things he says and does
to me and the way he makes me feel, so I pluck
up the courage, I'm gonna be more whale for
once in my life. I ring the bell, a few seconds
later, the door opens. Mrs. Alvin. Oh my God!
I nearly shit a cold purple Twinkie! My heart's
in my mouth, I'm beading with sweat all over.
This is not what I planned. "Hello?" she says -
and I'm gonna have to use my best womanly
voice right now. She turns out to be so sweet,
a kinda tiny lady with warm brown eyes and
soft hair, not like the hog monster I imagined
her to be. "Hello. I'm Frankie. I work for your
husband, and…" She cuts me off. "I know who

you are, son." That knocks me sideways. "Won't you come in? Don't worry, he's not home – he's at his Tuesday night 'business club'". I know then straight away, she knows all about "my husband and his so-called 'business' club, ever since a nice lady of color - you might know her? - stopped me a month ago by the eggplants in Albertsons, she filled me in. Didn't take long for me to connect the dots, let's put it that way, and I had him followed. I've always been a great fan of Columbo, turns out I'm a real life Jessica Fletcher. There's nothing I don't know about my Alvin." So, why don't she kick him out? "Timing, dear. A woman lives her life by the clock, so we're kinda experts at timing." This is an insight into the female brain I have absolutely no idea about. I tell her "I'm quitting, without notice". She smiles and then kisses me on the forehead, wishes me luck: "I've been sayin' my prayers for you. Oh, don't look so disgusted, son, I've not been prayin' to save your soul, I've been prayin' to save you from Alvin." Seems like her prayers have been answered, and I'm the living proof, a miracle. I thank her most sincerely and, as I'm about to take my leave, she reaches inside her store cupboard and pulls out a cheese grater. "I'll be making coleslaw tonight. When Alvin gets home". I swear her brown eyes turn red.

SCENE 19

Later the same night.
The twinkle lights in the trailer are lit dimly.
FRANKIE takes a beer from the refrigerator, cracks it open, sits on the crate and drinks with complete satisfaction. A moment of this to himself. After a moment, the door of the trailer opens slowly to reveal SHYANNE, wearing Anthony H. Froehlich's blood-stained jacket (which is too big for her) standing tragically - she has no will for anything and remains uncharacteristically calm/muted. Suddenly, FRANKIE realizes something is wrong and notices the blood.

FRANKIE: Shyanne, are you hurt?

SHYANNE: Only on the inside, kid.

FRANKIE: What happened? Look at you... Jeez, Shy,
          what the fuck!?

SHYANNE: ... There's been a commotion.

FRANKIE: A commotion? What kinda commotion?

SHYANNE: Kinda got the cloud on it right now. Can
          you please leave me, Frankie? I need
          some time to process things. Alone.

FRANKIE: I ain't going nowhere till you tell me exactly
          what's going on.

SHYANNE: I don't wanna talk about it. Like I said.

FRANKIE: What's happened here? You better start
          talking quick 'cos I'm supposed to be
          stuffing my bag with dreams.

SHYANNE: Is that so?

FRANKIE: Er, jer-jer-jer-jer, you're keeping something
          from me, and I bet it's to do with that contract.

SHYANNE: Contract?

FRANKIE: The new contract!

SHYANNE: Oh. There is no new contract.

FRANKIE: What the fuck happened to the new
          contract?

SHYANNE: Forget it.

FRANKIE: I already told you, I aint letting go of Vegas. Hang on a minute...

(He puts both index fingers mockingly to the side of his head with a dumb expression in his face)

Duh... Nope. That don't work. Got any other ideas I can try? Too late, 'cos we're goin' to Vegas! Vegas, Vegas, Vegas!

SHYANNE: Just shut up, you stupid little (faggot)...!

(Takes a deep breath)

Frankie, I need you to promise me you'll stay calm. 'Cos I'm gonna stay calm, nice and quiet, nice and calm for Shyanne, now.

FRANKIE: I don't wanna stay calm...

SHYANNE: You must, you gotta... 'Cos I got a confession. And Lord help me, it's a big one.

(SHYANNE takes holds of FRANKIE's hands and holds them tightly.)

He's dead.

(FRANKIE can't process this.)

Anthony. H Fröehlich, the Big Cheese I've been telling you about, the one with the so-called contract? He's dead.

FRANKIE: The Big Cheese is dead? Anthony H. Fröehlich

- is dead?

SHYANNE: Uh-huh. Dead. Do-do'd. Moved on to stiff

city... Say something, will you?

You're freaking me out.

FRANKIE: Froehlich's dead?

SHYANNE: That's right, kid. And it was me that killed

him.

(FRANKIE tries to scramble away from

this monstrous revelation, but SHYANNE

keeps a real hard grip.)

You ain't afraid of me, are you? 'Cos there

ain't nuttin' to be afraid of. This is Shyanne

talking, Momma Moonshine, you're still

my big boy, Frankie, nuttin's changed

between us, get what I'm saying?

(FRANKIE is terrified.)

Get what I'm saying?

(FRANKIE nods.)

Good man.

FRANKIE: You sure he's dead?

(SHYANNE mimes a knife across her

throat. He's dead all right.)

How? Why?

SHYANNE: Why? He got fresh, stupid!

FRANKIE: Fresh?

SHYANNE: Fresh! You gotta understand, there's fresh and there's fresh. You get what I'm saying on this one, I know you do. Well, maybe you don't, considering.

FRANKIE: Guys get fresh with you all the time, it's what you get paid for. None of this is making sense.

SHYANNE: I know, I know. But I kinda got a cloud on me right me now.

FRANKIE: Seems like you get the cloud too much lately!

SHYANNE: Fuck you, Frankie, he threatened me! With all sorts of violence against me. Guys like him make sure the likes of me will never work again, know what I'm saying? 'Cos nobody wants to see a face like that with deep scars staring right back at them from a pole. And men like him don't give a motherfuckin' fuck about washed up hos like me.

An awkward silence.

FRANKIE: Talk to me. What happened? With the contract?

SHYANNE: He had no intention whatsoever of signing

no contract, not Vegas, not Wichita,

not even Turtle Creek.

FRANKIE: Where is he now?

SHYANNE: Bottom of Miracle Lake, sleeping with the

fishes.

FRANKIE: The bottom of the lake?

SHYANNE: Uh-huh, in the trunk of my Chevvy. I'm

getting some clarity now, bear me out... that's

right, at some point he whipped out his

stubby little wiener, quicker than a rice rat.

I told him "put that thing right back where

it came from, I don't do tricks for free! I

need to feel the magic for that kinda thing."

And believe me, there weren't no magic.

FRANKIE: Did he put it away?

SHYANNE: Jerked off and then he spat. Right in my face.

FRANKIE: No way!

SHYANNE: It was still ok, 'cos I had me a plan.

FRANKIE: Was this a new plan or the old plan?

SHYANNE: A new plan.

FRANKIE: What was the new plan?

SHYANNE: The new plan was to give that low life

motherfucker one last chance

to change his mind.

FRANKIE: How?

SHYANNE: I pulled out my 22 from my purse...

FRANKIE: You got a 22?

SHYANNE: And I pointed it right at his balls. His dick

shrank to half its size, there and then.

Which ain't sayin' much. That's when I

gave him one hell of an ultimatum.

FRANKIE: What was it?

SHYANNE: Just hang in there. You gotta understand,

this is kinda emotional for me. I remember, I was

tellin' myself, "my dreams are disappearing down

the tubes by the second. Take the advantage,

Shyanne, you got this guy by the nuggets". If

I could just make my point reasonably, like,

he'd understand my position. And so I said...

FRANKIE: What?

SHYANNE: I said... you know what, I don't recall exactly
what I said. But I musta gone right off the
scale, yelling at the top of my voice, my
lungs were on fire, know what I'm saying?

FRANKIE: What did he do?

SHYANNE: *(matter of factly)*

Err... yeah, hang on, it's coming back
to me now, that's right, he called me...
"a knuckle dragging, no good nigger, no
hope ho, only fit for gator bait, the most
nigorant shit slinger he'd ever met" and...
oh yeah, I was a "liver lipped cunt".

FRANKIE: Oh, my God.

SHYANNE: My finger found its way inside the trigger
guard, he's yellin' at me all the time "you ain't
got the balls you ugly piece of nigger shit",
"you ape shit cunt", "cunt" and more "cunt",
he was in his flow. I was trying to reason with
him. Honest to God. And when I said you're
gonna be my Personal Assistant and the like -

FRANKIE: I am?

SHYANNE: Sure. Like we discussed, kid...

FRANKIE: We did?

SHYANNE: He called you a "freak".

FRANKIE: No way!

SHYANNE: At which point I discharged my weapon

without a second thought and I shot

him right in the brain bag.

(FRANKIE recoils.)

Followed by the head. And with that, all

my dreams were dead. And so was he.

(SHYANNE suddenly pulls herself together

and stands still, as if in a trance. She takes

a deep breath then reaches into her purse.

FRANKIE backs away rapidly, fearing she

is pulling out her gun. Instead she pulls out a

cigarette carton. She lights the cigarette. The

distant sound of police sirens getting closer.)

Listen, kid. I get it if...

FRANKIE: What?

SHYANNE: ... You need to run.

FRANKIE: Run?

SHYANNE: Jeez, Frankie!! Get outta here, go! And don't

look back. I'm two hundred and eighty in dog

years already. That's a lot of begging on my back legs for food. And both my heels just gave way.

FRANKIE: But -

SHYANNE: Go!

>*(A silence. Suddenly, FRANKIE turns, runs into the trailer and we hear sounds of frantic packing from within. SHYANNE, herself suddenly looking very tired, rubs her hair down, sighs and sits on a crate. She pulls out her makeup mirror and carefully starts to apply lip liner etc. FRANKIE emerges from the trailer with his knapsack and stares at SHYANNE with tears in his eyes. She ignores him. FRANKIE offers his red neckerchief but SHYANNE won't take it. FRANKIE gently places it in SHYANNE's lap. After a few moments, FRANKIE turns and runs. A beat.)*

Good man.

>*(After a moment or two, she turns her head skyward.)*

Poppa... if you can hear me...

(SHYANNE breaks down and sobs quietly,

wiping her eyes with Frankie's neckerchief.)

SCENE 20

10 minutes later.

FRANKIE returns quietly. He kneels down beside
her and takes her hand. SHYANNE, surprised but
also relieved, stares into his eyes, her own filled with
questions.

FRANKIE: *(tenderly)*

You gotta light?

SHYANNE: You gotta dick?

FRANKIE: I ain't going nowhere without you.

SHYANNE: *(wiping her eyes, crying but laughing, softly)*

You lame assed motherfuckin' retard,

you king mess, you know that, king

mess, that's what you are.

FRANKIE: That's me, just a nobody, pretending' to be a

nobody, but I'm your washed up guy, Shy.

SHYANNE: Why ain't you runnin' with the wind, kid?

FRANKIE: Why would I keep running? What am I

chasing? A new set of pecs, maybe buy me a
dick? What's the point, when I can't change this?

*(He points to his heart. SHYANNE smiles
and they embrace. A beat.)*

What happens now?

SHYANNE: ...I got me a plan.

FRANKIE: A plan? What kinda plan?

SHYANNE: The plan is - we're gonna drive, right over
the edge!

FRANKIE: But Shy, we ain't got a car no more. It's at the
bottom of the lake...

SHYANNE: Frankie, Frankie, Frankie, it's times like this,
you gotta believe, believe in miracles, like I do
in my voodoo and all its strange beauty. Look.
We got ourselves a Thunderbird convertible.

*SHYANNE leads FRANKIE to the two old movie
theater seats.*

FRANKIE: I don't get it. That ain't no car.

SHYANNE: In here it is.

Shyanne taps her head, sits and pats the empty seat beside her.

FRANKIE: ...Is it a stick shift?

SHYANNE: Whatever you want.

FRANKIE: I always wanted a stick shift. Them gear

boxes, they're so much more…

complicated. Got room for a dog?

SHYANNE: The biggest. Know what, kid, we already come

this far without wheels. And right now, we

got places to go.

FRANKIE: Like Vegas?

Frankie sits on the other seat.

SHYANNE: Like Vegas.

FRANKIE: I can't believe we're finally going to Vegas.

SHYANNE: Believe. It's just you and me, kid. Two scooters

under the same shell. You're all I got left.

Frankie, you sure you're ready to ride?

FRANKIE: Er, jer-jer-jer-jer!

SHYANNE: Good man. 'Cos I got me a plan.

*The twinkle lights on the trailer grow in brightness and bright
lights engulf SHYANNE and FRANKIE from behind.*

*Somewhere, we hear the sound of a heavy metal door
slamming.*

Blackout.

$Bw - 4/19.$